Written by **HEATHER FELLOWS**

illustrated by **CATARINA NETO**

Harper the Helper

Harper **LOOOOVED** to help.

She loved to help animals, and toys and other kids and lunch ladies. Helping was her favorite thing to do.

Before she left for school in the morning, she would help her daddy make his lunch for work.

"Daddy! Don't forget your extra pickles!"

When riding her bike to school with her big sister, Harper always looked for cars before crossing the road.

"Sis! Look out for that red truck!"

Harper would even help at school in her
1st grade classroom.

"Mrs. C, you dropped your pen!"

Even when it was time to be silent and everyone was busy learning, Harper would help in her quietest way.

"Isaac... let me help you with your shoe."

After school, Harper would help at soccer practice.

"Coach! I picked up the orange cones for you!"

And, she would help at softball practice too.

"Lucy! Don't forget your helmet!

Once Harper would get home from her long day, her mama would be setting the table for dinner. She would help even then!

"Mama, I've got the napkins!"

After dinner, when Harper was ready for bed, she would tell her mama all about the different ways she had helped people that day.

"Harper, my little helper, I'm so proud of your kind heart."

The Author...

Heather Fellows is a writer, mother, gardening enthusiast and business manager who makes reservations for dinner.

She holds her MBA from Friends University and puts those expensive skills to use by building spreadsheets that track sports fees, family finance and local takeout joints.

Most of her time is spent cheering on the sidelines of a ball field or watching reruns of the Golden Girls while folding obscene amounts of laundry.

Heather lives in Kansas with her charming husband, precocious three kids, and two dogs and two cats.

Made in the USA
Columbia, SC
31 January 2023

11310382R00018